HARRY THE HIPPO

HARRY'S Sandbox Surprise

Story by Nani Colorado
Illustrations by Jesús Gabán

Gareth Stevens Children's Books
MILWAUKEE

Today is a special day.
Daddy is taking Harry
to the park!

2

Harry walks right over to
the sandbox. "Hi, Barney.
May I play with you?"

"I'll let you play
with my fish . . .

4

. . . but only if you let
me have your star!"

Here comes Eddie.
"I have an idea! . . .

6

. . . Let's play King
of the Hill!"

"Okay, now what
should we do?"

8

Harry has an idea.

"Let's fill all the
pails with sand!"

10

"Okay. One, two,
three . . . whee!"

"Ow! It's in my eyes!"
"It's in my ears!"
"It's in my nose!
Ah choo!"

"Help, Daddy! I'm all
full of sand! I can
even taste it. Yuck!"

13

"Let's get you cleaned up.
It's too bad you didn't
have any fun here today,"
Daddy smiles.

14

"But Daddy, I had lots
of fun! Can we come
back tomorrow?"

15

For a free color catalog describing Gareth Stevens' list of high-quality children's books, call 1-800-341-3569 (USA) or 1-800-461-9120 (Canada).

Library of Congress Cataloging-in-Publication Data

Gabán, Jesús.
    [Papouf au tas de sable. English]
    Harry's sandbox surprise / written by Nani Colorado ; illustrated by
Jesús Gabán. -- North American ed.
        p. cm. -- (Harry the hippo)
    Translation of: Papouf au tas de sable / Jesús Gabán, Nani Colorado.
    Summary: Harry and his friends learn that there's a price to pay
when they throw sand at the playground.
    ISBN 0-8368-0716-2
    [1. Hippopotamus--Fiction. 2. Play--Fiction.] I. Colorado, Nani.
II. Title. III. Series: Gabán, Jesús. Harry the hippo.
PZ7.G1116Hat 1991
[E]—dc20   91-3219

North American edition first published in 1992 by

Gareth Stevens Children's Books
1555 North RiverCenter Drive, Suite 201
Milwaukee, Wisconsin 53212, USA

English text by Eileen Foran
Cover design by Beth Karpfinger and Sharone Burris

Printed in the United States of America

1 2 3 4 5 6 7 8 9 9 7 96 95 94 93 92